# Fuddles

To Jennifer, Julian, Meg, and Mary.
You are my little corner of the world.

ALADDIN

An imprint of Simon & Schuster Children's Publishing Division ● 1230 Avenue of the Americas, New York, NY 10020

First Aladdin hardcover edition May 2011 ● Text and illustrations copyright © 2011 by Frans Vischer

For information about special discounts for bulk purchases, please contact Simon & Schuster Special Sales

at 1-866-506-1949 or business@simonandschuster.com.

The Simon & Schuster Speakers Bureau can bring authors to your live event. For more information or to book an event

contact the Simon & Schuster Speakers Bureau at 1-866-248-3049 or visit our website at www.simonspeakers.com.

Designed by Karin Paprocki

The text of this book was set in Wade Sans Light.

The illustrations for this book were rendered digitally.

Manufactured in China

0211 SCP

2 4 6 8 10 9 7 5 3 1

Library of Congress Cataloging-in-Publication Data

Vischer, Frans.

Fuddles / written and illustrated by Frans Vischer. — 1st Aladdin hardcover ed. p. cm.

Summary: When Fuddles the cat escapes from his house and goes to explore the great outdoors, his adventure is more taxing than he expected it to be.

ISBN 978-1-4169-9155-7 (hardcover)

[1. Cats--Fiction.] I. Title. PZ7.V822Fu 2010 [E]--dc22 2010019049

# Fuddles

WRITTEN AND ILLUSTRATED BY Frans Vischer

Aladdin

NEW YORK   LONDON   TORONTO   SYDNEY

Fuddles was a fat,
pampered cat.

His family spoiled him.

And spoiled him.

And spoiled him.

One day, Fuddles realized that all he did was eat, sleep, and visit his litter box.

He decided that his life needed adventure. He was ready for a change. He summoned his courage and headed for the door.

But Mom had other ideas. "You're not allowed to go outside," she said.

*Mom said no?!* Fuddles could not believe his ears. He had never been told no in his life. Why couldn't he go outside now?

The lure of adventure had taken hold of him.

He dreamed of scaling soaring mountains and fighting ferocious foes. He was determined to go out.

Nothing was going to stop him.

To prepare for his grand adventure,
he started a strict exercise regimen.

(But not too strict.)

He practiced climbing.
He sharpened his
hunting skills—and his claws.

One lazy Sunday, Mom
told the kids to play outside.
This was his chance to escape!

Like a cheetah chasing a gazelle,
he made his speedy getaway.
He hoped Mom wouldn't notice!

Once outside, Fuddles got right down
to business. He'd show those
birds who was boss!

But last night's pork chops weighed him down.

Fuddles landed in the most disgusting bath
he'd ever had. He wondered if anybody ever
cleaned around here——Mom always kept his
home spotless.

As he washed himself, he heard laughter from above.
Messes weren't funny. He'd show those squirrels who would
have the last laugh!

He pushed and pulled, and strained and struggled, and then he realized that couches were easier to climb than trees. Perhaps he should've practiced a little more first. . . .

Fuddles was worn out. He needed a break from adventure. A short catnap in the neighbor's yard was in order.

. . . a very short catnap.

Fuddles thought it best not to use his fighting skills at the moment. This dog looked like he meant business.

He began to think he
wasn't cut out for adventure.
He didn't even know how
he'd get down from the tree.

What a landing! Fuddles tried to get out of there quick,
but he found himself stuck.

   His training hadn't prepared him for this at all!
He went up and down, and back and forth,
and up and down again.

And then he just went down.
He was left a little dizzy, and he had an
upset tummy. Plus, he needed his litter box.

He wasn't sure where he was. But he was scared
and lonely and wanted to go home.

Nothing around him looked familiar.
The only thing he could do was go search
for his house, and his family.

It was getting darker and darker——and Fuddles
was getting more and more scared. He missed his
family terribly. He hoped they missed him, too.

Plus, his tummy was rumbling.
Suddenly his ears pricked up.
What's that noise? It was coming closer.

It was his family calling him!

Finally, some friendly, familiar faces! He was so happy to see them!

Back at home, Fuddles realized that this was truly where he belonged.
And all great adventurers deserve to be pampered.